The Ugly Five

By Julia Donaldson

ALISON
GREEN
BOOKS

Illustrated by Axel Scheffler

Morning had dawned on the African plain.
The lion lay grooming his glorious mane.
The kudu looked cool and the rhino looked fine.
The bright pink flamingos looked simply divine.
The zebra looked graceful; the leopard looked great.

Oh, what a picture of beauty – but wait!

Who is this creature so ugly and weird
With her spindly legs and her gingery beard?
With her big chunky chest and her skinny behind,
To say she looks plain would be really quite kind.

It's the wildebeest! Slowly she ambled along,
Trampling the grasses and singing this song:

"I'm the ugly one, I'm the ugly one.
I'm the ugliest animal under the sun.
My ungainly appearance is second to none.
I'm the ugly one, I'm the ugly one . . .

"But here's someone uglier even than me!
Who can this strange-looking specimen be?"

"How do you do? I'm the spotted hyena.
Who could be uglier? Who could look meaner?
My mane is all spiky, my skin is all spotty.
No other creature could look quite so grotty.
My voice is a mixture of giggles and groans,
And I like nothing better than crunching on bones.
I must be the ugliest beast in the scrub."

Then the wildebeest shouted . . .

"Hurrah! Join the club."

The two ugly animals ambled along,
Kicking the dust up and singing this song:

"We're the ugly two, we're the ugly two.
We wouldn't win prizes for beauty, it's true.
You'll see nothing worse if you go to the zoo.
We're the ugly two, we're the ugly two . . .

"But who is this hideous bird we can see,
Perched on a branch of the powder-puff tree?"

"I'm the lappet-faced vulture. I'm ugly and bald.
No wonder that everyone looks so appalled.
I have flaps on my face that are wrinkled and pink,
My beak is gigantic and, what's more, I stink.
At mealtimes my habits are really quite vile:
I much prefer food that's been dead for a while.
I'm clearly a lot more revolting than you."

Then the other two shouted . . .

"Bravo! Join the crew!"

The three ugly animals ambled along,
Splashing through water and singing this song:

"We're the ugly three, we're the ugly three,
The ugliest beasts that you're likely to see.
You wouldn't be tempted to ask us to tea.
We're the ugly three, we're the ugly three . . .

"But who is this animal having a roll
In the bubbling mud of the watering hole?"

"Hello! I'm the warthog, as ugly as sin,
With two pairs of tusks and a bristly chin.
My tail stands on end and my body is dumpy.
My head is too big and my skin is too bumpy.
People are shocked by my deafening snorts
And my face that is covered in horrible warts.
I'm the worst-looking creature from here to Japan."

Then the other three shouted . . .

"Yippee! Join the clan!"

The four ugly animals ambled along,
Scaring the starlings and singing this song:

"We're the ugly four, we're the ugly four.
We're grisly and gruesome and hard to ignore.
Take just one look and your eyes will feel sore.
We're the ugly four, we're the ugly four . . .

"But who is this perfectly terrible frump,
Raiding the rubbish bins down by the dump?"

"I'm the marabou stork, and I think you'll agree
That no other bird looks as dreadful as me.
My wings are enormous, I'm hunched and I'm gangly,
And look at my throat pouch – it's all dingly-dangly.
My legs, long and skinny, are covered in poo,
And I'll eat almost anything, even a shoe.
I'm a grouchy old grump. I'm a horrible slob."

Then the other four shouted . . .

"Yoo-hoo! Join the mob!"

So the five ugly animals ambled along,
Casting long shadows and singing this song:

"We're the ugly five, we're the ugly five.
Everyone flees when they see us arrive.
How can such hideous creatures survive?
We're the ugly five, we're the ugly five . . .

"But, stop!
        Just a minute . . .
            Be quiet.
                Who are these,
                    Peeping from burrows,
                        and hiding in trees?"

"Hello! We're your babies. You give us our food,

And help cheer us up when we're in a bad mood.

You clean us and preen us and pick out the nits,

And we want you to know that we love you to bits.

We love all your spots and your warts and your bristles,

Your grunts and your groans and your hoots and your whistles.

We really don't think you look ugly at all.

You're beauties! You're bombshells! The belles of the ball.

"You're kind and you're cuddly, you're brave and you're strong,

And that is our reason for singing this song:

"You're the lovely five, you're the lovely five.
You're sweeter than honey from bees in a hive.
You're quite the most beautiful creatures alive –

"You're the lovely five,
You're the lovely five."

If you went on safari, which animals would you like to see?

Perhaps you'd like to meet the **Big Five**? They're very grand, but they're the most dangerous animals on the savannah:

You could try and spot the **Little Five.** Their names are similar to the Big Five, but they're all very small:

Lion

Buffalo Weaver

Leopard

Leopard Tortoise

Rhinoceros

Ant Lion

Buffalo

Rhinoceros Beetle

Elephant

Elephant Shrew

You'd have to be very lucky to see the **Shy Five.** They mostly only come out at night, and are very good at hiding:

Or how about the **Ugly Five?** Some people say they're the ugliest animals in Africa. Others think they're just gorgeous. What do you think?

Aardvark

Lappet-Faced Vulture

 Porcupine

 Spotted Hyena

Aardwolf

Wildebeest

 Meerkat

 Marabou Stork

Bat-Eared Fox

Warthog

For ranger Lucky
and tracker Charlie – J.D.

First published in the UK in 2017 by
Alison Green Books
An imprint of Scholastic Children's Books
Euston House, 24 Eversholt Street
London NW1 1DB, UK
A division of Scholastic Ltd
www.scholastic.co.uk
London – New York – Toronto – Sydney – Auckland
Mexico City – New Delhi – Hong Kong

Text copyright © 2017 Julia Donaldson
Illustrations copyright © 2017 Axel Scheffler

HB ISBN: 978 1 407174 19 8

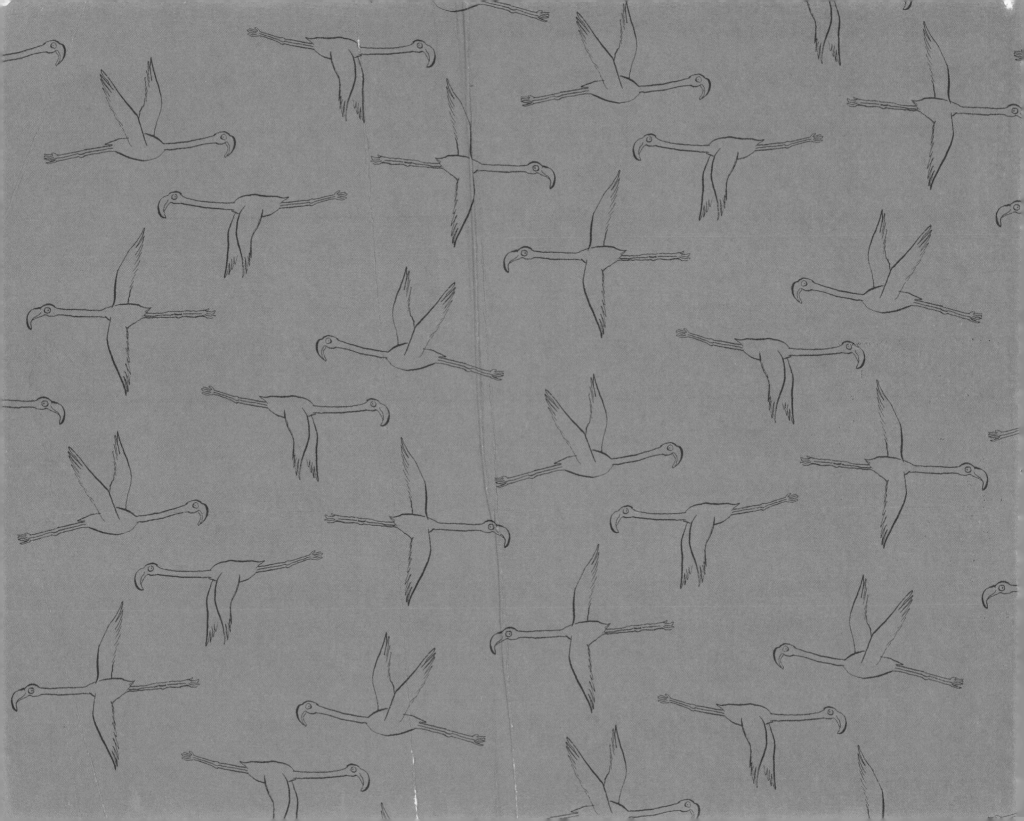